JOURNEY OF JAMES FROM ROAD TO SPACE

TANAY SHAH

Contents

Contents

PREFACE

This story proves that doing hard work always shows results. You should never give up. You should always make your weakness as your strength, as here James had to sell newspaper but he mentally conceived the Bright side so he read the newspaper and noted down the space news. After he worked hard he joined NASA. Throughout his mission he never gave up, he tried and tried until he succeeded.

"Dream Big. stay positive, work hard and enjoy the journey" By Urijah Faber

I

Chapter 1:- About James

"Once in New York, USA there lived a boy named James Williams. His studies were at the New York High School. He lived in New York, USA. Astronomy, i.e. The study of the universe, was his passion. As a result of his family's poverty, he sold newspapers. He carried a small notebook while reading newspapers and if there were any space-related news, he would write the details down and read them at home. Each time he received pocket money from his parents, he would purchase a space book at the bookstore. When he finished reading the book and had noted down important points in his same notebook, he would sell it and buy another book. During his school space science class, his teacher, Miss Jessica asked a question to the whole class, "What is the closest Black Hole to Earth?" James raises his hand. "Yes, James", his teacher said. James replied, "Unicorn Black Hole,

it's the smallest, too."Miss Jessica then asked, "Do you know the largest black hole too?" James replies, "Yes, it's TON 618." "Can I tell you something about it?" Miss Jessica responded. "Yes, you may,". James said "The galaxy in which we live, which is the Milky Way galaxy, has a Supermassive black hole at its center called Sagittarius A," said James. "Thank you, James," replied Miss Jessica. "Welcome," announced James."*

II

Chapter 2:- Space Olympiad

*"His denomination was **Fred**. One day in school, Miss Jessica asked who will participate in **Space Olympiad**. Everyone gave their designations. Even Fred gave his designation. Then James came in, "May I come in mam?" He verbally expressed gasping the air expeditiously. She verbalized "yes". She called him to her and asked "Why were you late today". She was very irate and chastised him deplorably. James verbalized "I was selling newspapers." After aurally perceiving this she was shocked and took him to the staff. When they were going to the staff, all the other students were laughing at him. In the staff, he verbalized why he worked as a newspaper vendor. Then Miss Jessica asked, "Do you want to participate in the Space Olympiad"? He verbalized, "Yes, I want to participate too". After hearing that James was giving*

the Olympiad, everyone commence teasing him that a newspaper vendor will never be able to win this Olympiad. Just after some weeks prospering the exam in the list, James was ***first*** *and Fred was in* ***third****. By optically discerning this Fred was very exasperated. James made his family proud and jubilant. His mother made some sweets and his father bought his favorite thing in the world is* ***Space Encyclopedia****."*

III

Chapter 3:- James Journey to NASA

"He passed 10th and 12th and got 98% and 99% respectively. At the age of 20, he asked his parents to buy a telescope. His father was a Farmer. So, on his birthday, his father sold his cycle and gifted him a telescope. As soon as he realized that his father had sold his cycle for the telescope, he searched for information on NASA and how to work as a NASA scientist using his mobile phone (which he had received as a gift). With hard work and dedication, he became a NASA scientist. He was very blissful. His parents appreciated his effort"

NASA

IV

Chapter 4:- About the James mission on Mars

"James made a plan for a mission to Mars. It occurred to him that we could launch a rocket that carries an orbiter that carries three Landers. One will go to Mars and the other 2 will go to its moons. Rovers will leave the Lander to search for water and oxygen, which are both valuable resources. The seniors agreed with the plan. Within two months, the rocket, orbiter, Lander, and the rover were ready. However, when they launched the rocket, it flew a little and crashed at the launch site. Two more attempts were made, but neither was successful."

V

Chapter 5:- About the success of James in his mission to Mars

"Everyone gave up, but James said, "We can do it if we try once more." After watching his courage and confidence, everyone accepted it when they tried one last time. And they succeeded. The rocket when into space and reached Mars, there the orbiter came out and the Lander came out from the orbiter and flew down to the surface of Mars and the rover came out when the Lander landed on Mars. Once the orbiter has reached both Martian moons Phobos and Deimos, it released the Lander, which flew down to the surface of each moon, and the rover followed after the Lander landed. It was called the Mars Orbit

Satellite (MOS) because it orbited the entire Mars orbit."

This was his mission to Mars

VI

Chapter 6:- About the James mission on Proxima Centauri b

"After Succeeding in the MOS mission He planned to send a rocket containing a satellite to Proxima Centauri b in the Alpha Centauri System. It is a habitable exoplanet. He named it "Proxima Centauri Satellite (PCS)"Within one month, the rocket, and the satellite were ready. The satellite's main mission was to find any life existence, Water and Oxygen on Proxima Centauri b. However, when they launched the rocket, it flew a little and crashed at the launch site. Three more attempts were made, but neither was successful."

VII

Chapter 7:- About James's success in his mission on Proxima Centauri b

"A last-ditch effort was successful. It took some years for the rocket to reach Proxima Centauri b. The rocket flew at 1/20 the speed of light, so it took very little time. It was the fastest spacecraft ever. There the satellite came out and commenced to revolve around the exoplanet. It sent every information to the Earth. Everyone appreciated him."

This was his mission to Proxima Centauri b

VIII

Chapter 8:- About the James mission onKepler 452b

"After the PCS mission was successful, he planned to launch a rocket with a satellite to Kepler 452b in The Kepler-452 planetary system. This is also an earthlike planet. It was named Kepler 452b Satellite (K452bS) Within 1.5 months, the rocket and satellite were ready. Kepler 452b's primary mission was to find life, water, and oxygen. IIowever, when they launched the rocket, it flew a little and crashed near the launch Despite further attempts, there was no success."

IX

Chapter 9:- About James's success in his mission on Kepler 452b

"Last-ditch efforts succeeded. The rocket reached Kepler 452b some years after launch. Rockets travel at 1/15 the speed of light, so it took very little time. The satellite emerged and began to orbit the exoplanet. It transmitted every piece of information to Earth. He was appreciated by all again."

This was his mission to Kepler 452b

X

Chapter 10:- About the James mission on Stephenson 2-18

"Following the successful launch of K452bS, he planned to launch a rocket with a satellite to Stephenson 2-18 in the constellation Scutum. Since he had just sent satellites to planets and exoplanets, he decided to send them to stars. Stephenson 2-18 (The largest star in the universe) had been his mission since his childhood. So he built a satellite that was fire and heat-proof. The satellite was named Stephenson 2-18 Satellite (S18S) and the rocket was ready within 2.5 months. They launched the rocket, but it flew just a little and crashed near the launch site.Despite further attempts, the mission did not succeed."

XI

Chapter 11:- About James's success in his mission on Stephenson 2-18

"Success was achieved with a last-ditch effort. Several years after launch, the rocket reached Stephenson 2-18 Rockets travel at 1/10 the speed of light, so it took very little time to get there. The satellite entered orbit and commenced its mission. Information was transferred to Earth throughout the mission. He was once again appreciated by everyone."

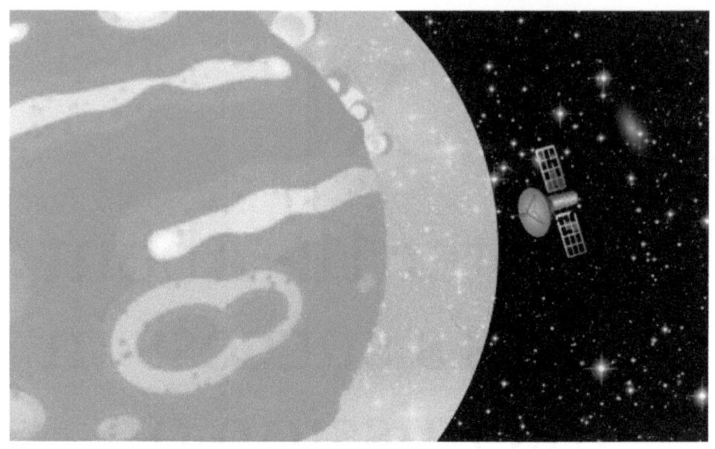

This was his mission to Stephenson 2-18

XII

Chapter 12- About the James mission on Proxima Centauri

"Following the successful launch of S18S, he planned to launch a rocket with a satellite to Proxima Centauri in the constellation Alpha Centauri. Proxima Centauri (The closest star to the Earth after Sun). So he built a satellite that was fire and heat-proof too. The satellite was named Proxima Centauri Star Satellite (PCSS) and the rocket was ready within 2.5 months. They launched the rocket, but it flew just a little and crashed near the launch site. Despite further attempts, the mission did not succeed."

XIII

Chapter 13:- About the James mission on Proxima Centauri

"A last-ditch effort led to success. The rocket reached Proxima Centauri, several years after launch. Rockets travel at about one-tenth of the speed of light, so it took very little time to reach the star. The satellite entered orbit and commenced its mission. During the mission, information was transferred to Earth. He was once again praised by everyone."

This was his mission to Proxima Centauri

XIV

Chapter 14-About the James mission on Sirius

"After the success of PCSS, he planned to launch a rocket with a satellite to Sirius (the brightest star in the night sky). He designed a satellite that was both fireproof and heat proof. In two months, the Sirius Star Satellite (SSS) was ready, and the rocket was launched. However, the rocket flew just a few feet, then crashed near the launch site. Despite further attempts, the mission did not succeed."

XV

Chapter 15:- About James's success in his mission to Sirius

"A final attempt was made, and they succeeded. The rocket reached Sirius several years after launch. Rockets travel at approximately one-tenth the speed of light, so it took very little time for the satellite to enter orbit and begin its mission. During the mission, information was transferred to Earth. He was once again praised by everyone. Then he went on many more missions and succeeded in each one."

This was his mission to Sirius

9 798886 295818

Printed by Libri Plureos GmbH in Hamburg, Germany